W9-DDM-006

TREASURY
OF
NURSERY
RHYMES

ERIC AND LUCY KINCAID'S
TREASURY
OF
NURSERY
RHYMES

BRIMAX BOOKS

Cambridge — England

Contents

To children everywhere:

As you look through the pages of this book, you will find many nursery rhymes which you already know. How is it that you came to know or learn them, perhaps even before you could read?

For hundreds and hundreds of years, mothers have sung songs and recited verses to their children when they were very young. Many of these songs and verses were first made up by children at play, some were made up by grown-ups for themselves, others are tongue-twisters, nonsense rhymes, lullabies and jingles which are so old no one knows where they came from.

When children grow up, they recite or sing the same songs or verses to *their* children and so they are handed down from one generation to another. This is why they are called 'traditional'.

This book is a collection of old and new verses and songs which have come to be known today as NURSERY RHYMES.

Turn the pages, the more you read the more you will remember: the more you look at the pictures the more you will see.

This book is for you to treasure always.

ISBN 0 86112 028 0
© Brimax Rights Ltd. 1981. All rights reserved
Published by Brimax Books, Cambridge, England 1981.
Some of the rhymes and illustrations in this
collection appear in "Just For You Nursery Rhymes";
"Every Day Nursery Rhymes"; "Tell Me
More Nursery Rhymes"; and "Listen and Say
Nursery Rhymes" also published by Brimax Books.
Third Printing 1983
Printed in Belgium

One, two, three, four,
Mary at the cottage door,
Five, six, seven, eight,
Eating cherries off a plate.

Mary had a little lamb,
It's fleece was white as snow;
And everywhere that Mary went
The lamb was sure to go.

It followed her to school one day,
That was against the rule;
It made the children laugh and play
To see a lamb at school.

And so the teacher turned it out,
But still it lingered near,
And waited patiently about
Till Mary did appear.

Why does the lamb love Mary so?
The eager children cry;
Why, Mary loves the lamb, you know,
The teacher did reply.

Hickety, pickety, my black hen,
She lays eggs for gentlemen;
Gentlemen come every day
To see what my black hen doth lay.
Sometimes nine and sometimes ten,
Hickety, pickety, my black hen.

For want of a nail the shoe was lost,
For want of a shoe the horse was lost,
For want of a horse the rider was lost,
For want of a rider the battle was lost,
For want of a battle the kingdom was lost,
And all for the want of a horseshoe nail.

There was a little woman,
As I have heard tell,
She went to market
Her eggs for to sell;
She went to market
All on a market day,
And she fell asleep
On the king's highway.

There came by a pedlar,
His name was Stout,
He cut her petticoats
All round about;
He cut her petticoats
Up to her knees;
Which made the little woman
To shiver and sneeze.

When this little woman
Began to awake,
She began to shiver,
And she began to shake;
She began to shake,
And she began to cry,
Lawk a mercy on me,
This is none of I!

But if this be I,
As I do hope it be,
I have a little dog at home
And he knows me;
If it be I,
He'll wag his little tail,
And if it be not I
He'll loudly bark and wail!

Home went the little woman
All in the dark,
Up starts the little dog,
And he began to bark;
He began to bark,
And she began to cry,
Lawk a mercy on me,
This is none of I!

Pussy cat Mole jumped over a coal
And in her best petticoat burnt a great hole.
Poor pussy's weeping, she'll have no more milk
Until her best petticoat's mended with silk.

Goosey, goosey gander,
Whither shall I wander?
Upstairs and downstairs
And in my lady's chamber.
There I met an old man
Who would not say his prayers.
I took him by the left leg
And threw him down the stairs.

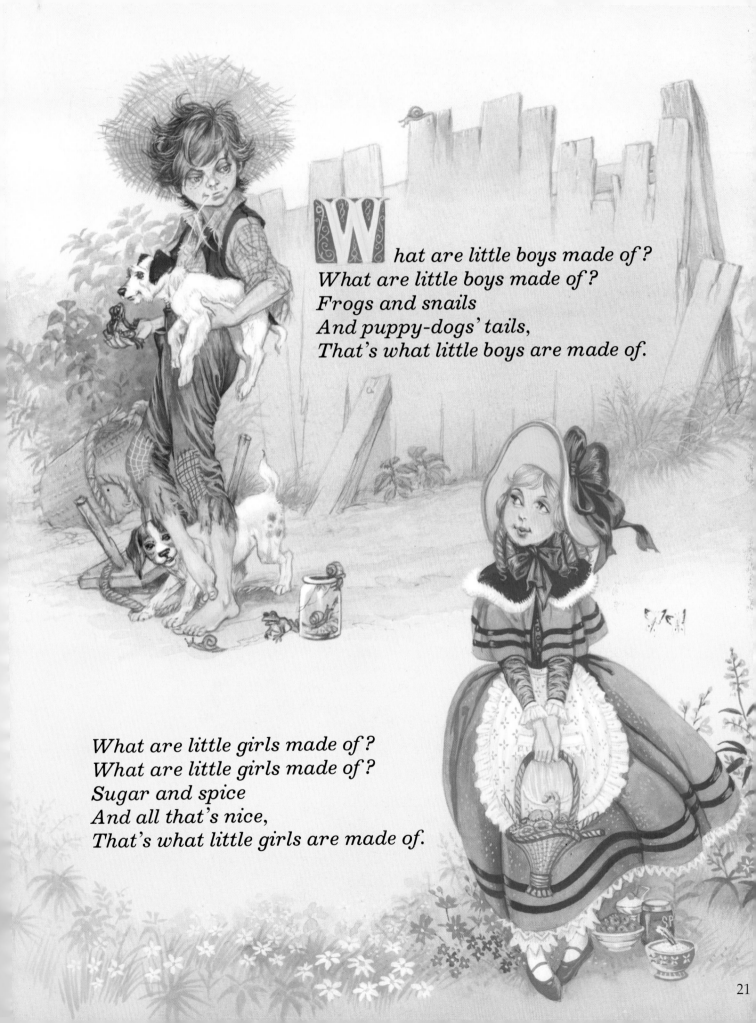

What are little boys made of?
What are little boys made of?
Frogs and snails
And puppy-dogs' tails,
That's what little boys are made of.

What are little girls made of?
What are little girls made of?
Sugar and spice
And all that's nice,
That's what little girls are made of.

*L*ondon Bridge is broken down,
Broken down, broken down,
London Bridge is broken down,
My fair lady.

Build it up with wood and clay,
Wood and clay, wood and clay,
Build it up with wood and clay,
My fair lady.

Wood and clay will wash away,
Wash away, wash away,
Wood and clay will wash away,
My fair lady.

Build it up with bricks and mortar,
Bricks and mortar, bricks and mortar,
Build it up with bricks and mortar,
My fair lady.

Bricks and mortar will not stay,
Will not stay, will not stay,
Bricks and mortar will not stay,
My fair lady.

Build it up with iron and steel,
Iron and steel, iron and steel,
Build it up with iron and steel,
My fair lady.

Iron and steel will bend and bow,
Bend and bow, bend and bow,
Iron and steel will bend and bow,
My fair lady.

Build it up with silver and gold,
Silver and gold, silver and gold,
Build it up with silver and gold,
My fair lady.

Silver and gold will be stolen away,
Stolen away, stolen away,
Silver and gold will be stolen away,
My fair lady.

Set a man to watch all night,
Watch all night, watch all night,
Set a man to watch all night,
My fair lady.

Suppose the man should fall asleep,
Fall asleep, fall asleep,
Suppose the man should fall asleep?
My fair lady.

Give him a pipe to smoke all night,
Smoke all night, smoke all night,
Give him a pipe to smoke all night,
My fair lady.

24

O f all the gay birds that e'er I did see,
The owl is the fairest by far to me,
For all day long she sits on a tree,
And when the night comes away flies she.

R ide a cock-horse to Banbury Cross,
To buy little Johnny a galloping horse;
It trots behind and it ambles before,
And Johnny shall ride till he can ride no more.

hree blind mice, see how they run!
They all ran after the farmer's wife,
Who cut off their tails with a carving knife,
Did you ever see such a thing in your life,
As three blind mice?

27

Little Robin Redbreast sat upon a tree,
Up went pussy cat, and down went she;
Down came pussy, and away Robin ran;
Says little Robin Redbreast, Catch me if you can.
Little Robin Redbreast jumped upon a wall,
Pussy cat jumped after him, and almost got a fall;
Little Robin chirped and sang, and what did pussy say?
Pussy cat said, Mew, and Robin jumped away.

Old King Cole
Was a merry old soul,
And a merry old soul was he;
He called for his pipe,
And he called for his bowl,
And he called for his fiddlers three.

Every fiddler, he had a fiddle,
And a very fine fiddle had he;
Twee tweedle dee, tweedle dee, went the fiddlers.
Oh, there's none so rare
As can compare
With King Cole and his fiddlers three.

29

Ring the bells, ring!
Hip, hurrah for the King!
The dunce fell into the pool, oh!
The dunce was going to school, oh!
The groom and the cook
Fished him out with a hook,
And he piped his eye like a fool, oh!

As I was going to Banbury,
Upon a summer's day,
My dame had butter, eggs, and fruit,
And I had corn and hay;
Joe drove the ox, and Tom the swine,
Dick took the foal and mare,
I sold them all — then home to dine,
From famous Banbury fair.

There was an old woman
Lived under a hill,
And if she's not gone
She lives there still.

How many miles to Babylon?
Three score miles and ten.
Can I get there by candle-light?
Yes, and back again.
If your heels are nimble and light,
You may get there by candle-light.

Hush-a-bye, baby, on the tree top,
When the wind blows the cradle will rock;
When the bough breaks the cradle will fall,
Down will come baby, cradle, and all.

Doctor Foster went to Gloucester
In a shower of rain;
He stepped in a puddle,
Right up to his middle,
And never went there again.

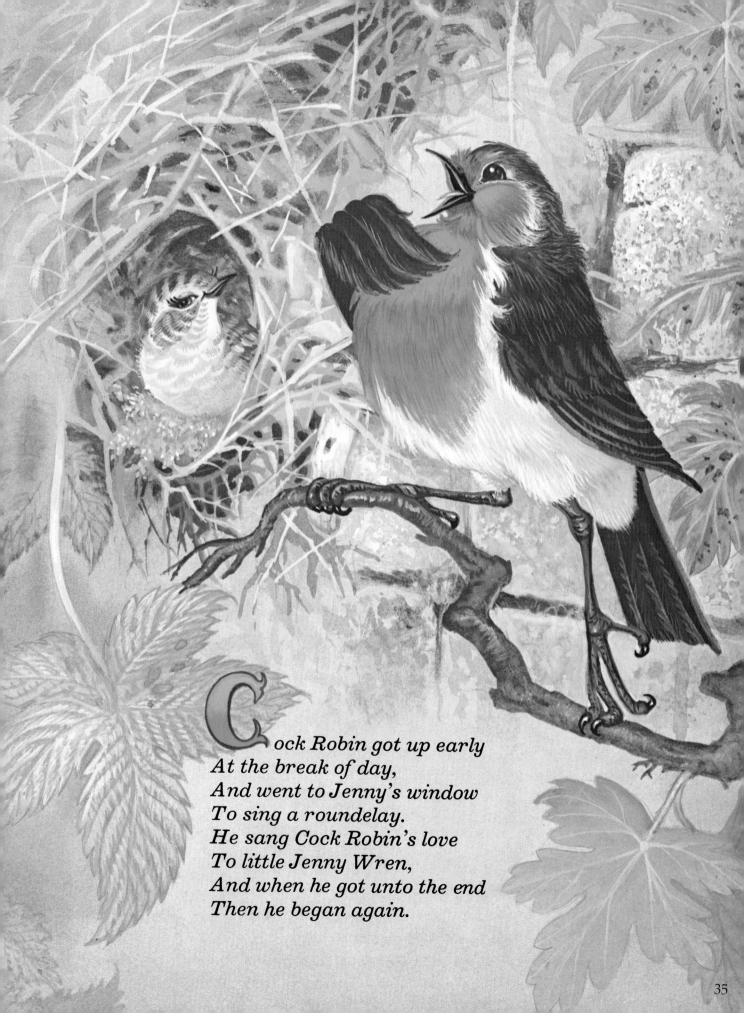

Cock Robin got up early
At the break of day,
And went to Jenny's window
To sing a roundelay.
He sang Cock Robin's love
To little Jenny Wren,
And when he got unto the end
Then he began again.

Old Mother Twitchett has but one eye,
And a long tail which she can let fly,
And every time she goes over a gap,
She leaves a bit of her tail in a trap.

Three little kittens they lost their mittens,
And they began to cry,
Oh, mother dear, we sadly fear
That we have lost our mittens.
What! LOST YOUR MITTENS, YOU NAUGHTY KITTENS.
Then you shall have no pie.
Mee-ow, mee-ow, mee-ow.
No, you shall have no pie.

The three little kittens they found their mittens,
And they began to cry,
Oh, mother dear, see here, see here,
For we have found our mittens.
Put on your mittens, you silly kittens,
And you shall have some pie.
Purr-r, purr-r, purr-r,
Oh, let us have some pie.

The three little kittens put on their mittens,
And soon ate up the pie;
Oh, mother dear, we greatly fear
That we have soiled our mittens.
What! soiled your mittens, you naughty kittens!
Then they began to sigh.
Mee-ow, mee-ow, mee-ow.
Then they began to sigh.

The three little kittens they washed their mittens,
And hung them out to dry;
Oh! mother dear, do you not hear
That we have washed our mittens?
What! washed your mittens, then you're good kittens,
But I smell a rat close by.
Mee-ow, mee-ow, mee-ow.
We smell a rat close by.

In a cottage in Fife
Lived a man and his wife,
Who, believe me, were comical folk;
For, to people's surprise,
They both saw with their eyes,
And their tongues moved whenever they spoke!
When quite fast asleep,
I've been told that to keep
Their eyes open they could not contrive;
They walked on their feet,
And 'twas thought what they ate
Helped, with drinking, to keep them alive!

39

Dickery, dickery, dare,
The pig flew up in the air;
The man in brown soon brought him down,
Dickery, dickery, dare.

Curly locks, Curly locks,
Wilt thou be mine?
Thou shalt not wash dishes
Nor yet feed the swine,
But sit on a cushion
And sew a fine seam,
And feed upon strawberries,
Sugar and cream.

Peter White will ne'er go right;
Would you know the reason why?
He follows his nose wherever he goes,
And that stands all awry.

The old woman must stand at the tub, tub, tub,
The dirty clothes to rub, rub, rub;
But when they are clean, and fit to be seen,
She'll dress like a lady, and dance on the green.

The cock crows in the morn
To tell us to rise,
And he that lies late
Will never be wise:
For early to bed,
And early to rise,
Is the way to be healthy
And wealthy and wise.

Dance to your daddy,
My little babby,
Dance to your daddy, my little lamb;
You shall have a fishy
In a little dishy,
You shall have a fishy when the boat comes in.

O ld chairs to mend! Old chairs to mend!
I never would cry old chairs to mend,
If I'd as much money as I could spend,
I never would cry old chairs to mend.

Old clothes to sell! Old clothes to sell!
I never would cry old clothes to sell,
If I'd as much money as I could tell,
I never would cry old clothes to sell.

One, two, three, four, five,
Once I caught a fish alive,
Six, seven, eight, nine, ten,
Then I let it go again.

Why did you let it go?
Because it bit my finger so.
Which finger did it bite?
This little finger on the right.

I love little pussy,
Her coat is so warm,
And if I don't hurt her
She'll do me no harm.
So I'll not pull her tail,
Nor drive her away,
But pussy and I
Very gently will play.

The man in the moon
Came down too soon,
And asked his way to Norwich;
He went by the south,
And burnt his mouth
With supping cold plum porridge.

46

Bye, baby bunting,
Daddy's gone a-hunting,
Gone to get a rabbit skin
To wrap the baby bunting in.

47

When I was a little girl,
About seven years old,
I hadn't got a petticoat,
To keep me from the cold.

So I went into Darlington,
That pretty little town,
And there I bought a petticoat,
A cloak, and a gown.

I went into the woods
And built me a kirk,
And all the birds of the air,
They helped me to work.

The hawk, with his long claws,
Pulled down the stone,
The dove, with her rough bill,
Brought me them home.

The parrot was the clergyman,
The peacock was the clerk,
The bullfinch played the organ,
And we made merry work.

49

If all the seas were one sea,
What a great sea that would be!
If all the trees were one tree,
What a great tree that would be!
And if all the axes were one axe,
What a great axe that would be!
And if all the men were one man,
What a great man that would be!
And if the great man took the great axe,
And cut down the great tree,
And let it fall into the great sea,
What a splish-splash that would be!

Lavender's blue, diddle, diddle,
Lavender's green;
When I am king, diddle, diddle,
You shall be queen.

Call up your men, diddle, diddle,
Set them to work,
Some to the plough, diddle, diddle,
Some to the cart.

Some to make hay, diddle, diddle,
Some to thresh corn,
Whilst you and I, diddle, diddle,
Keep ourselves warm.

Tom, he was a piper's son,
He learnt to play when he was young,
And all the tune that he could play
Was, 'Over the hills and far away';
Over the hills and a great way off,
The wind shall blow my top-knot off.

Tom with his pipe made such a noise,
That he pleased both the girls and boys,
And they all stopped to hear him play,
'Over the hills and far away'.

Tom with his pipe did play with such skill
That those who heard him could never keep still;
As soon as he played they began for to dance,
Even pigs on their hind legs would after him prance.

As Dolly was milking her cow one day,
Tom took his pipe and began to play;
So Doll and the cow danced 'The Cheshire Round',
Till the pail was broken and the milk
ran on the ground.

He met old Dame Trot with a basket of eggs,
He used his pipe and she used her legs;
She danced about till the eggs were all broke,
She began for to fret, but he laughed at the joke.

Tom saw a cross fellow was beating an ass,
Heavy laden with pots, pans, dishes, and glass;
He took out his pipe and he played them a tune,
And the poor donkey's load was
lightened full soon.

Jack and Jill went up the hill
To fetch a pail of water;
Jack fell down and broke his crown,
And Jill came tumbling after.

Up Jack got, and home did trot,
As fast as he could caper,
To old Dame Dob, who patched his nob
With vinegar and brown paper.

54

Diddlety, diddlety, dumpty,
The cat ran up the plum tree;
Half a crown
To fetch her down,
Diddlety, diddlety, dumpty.

Elsie Marley is grown so fine,
She won't get up to feed the swine,
But lies in bed till eight or nine.
Lazy Elsie Marley.

55

Cross-patch,
Draw the latch,
Sit by the fire and spin;
Take a cup,
And drink it up,
Then call your neighbours in.

The cock's on the wood pile a-blowing his horn,
The bull's in the barn a-threshing of corn,
The maids in the meadows are making the hay,
The ducks in the river are swimming away.

57

ittle Johnny Morgan,
Gentleman of Wales,
Came riding on a nanny-goat,
Selling of pigs' tails.

Upon Paul's steeple stands a tree
As full of apples as may be;
The little boys of London town
They run with hooks to pull them down:
And then they go from hedge to hedge
Until they come to London Bridge.

Lucy Locket lost her pocket,
Kitty Fisher found it;
Not a penny was there in it,
Only ribbon round it.

Come, let's to bed,
Says Sleepy-head;
Tarry a while, says Slow;
Put on the pot,
Says Greedy-gut,
We'll sup before we go.

Little Tommy Tittlemouse
Lived in a little house;
He caught fishes
In other men's ditches.

Oh, the brave old Duke of York,
He had ten thousand men;
He marched them up to the top of the hill,
And he marched them down again.
And when they were up, they were up,
And when they were down, they were down
And when they were only half-way up,
They were neither up nor down.

Simple Simon met a pieman,
Going to the fair;
Says Simple Simon to the pieman,
Let me taste your ware.

Says the pieman to Simple Simon,
Show me first your penny;
Says Simple Simon to the pieman
Indeed I have not any.

Simple Simon went a-fishing,
For to catch a whale;
All the water he had got
Was in his mother's pail.

Simple Simon went to look
If plums grew on a thistle;
He pricked his fingers very much,
Which made poor Simon whistle.

He went for water in a sieve
But soon it all fell through;
And now poor Simple Simon
Bids you all adieu.

Betty Botter bought some butter,
But, she said, the butter's bitter;
If I put it in my batter
It will make my batter bitter,
But a bit of better butter
Will make my batter better.
So she bought a bit of butter
Better than her bitter butter,
And she put it in her batter
And the batter was not bitter.
So 'twas better Betty Botter
bought a bit of better butter.

There were three jovial Welshmen,
As I have heard men say,
And they would go a-hunting
Upon St. David's Day.

All the day they hunted
And nothing could they find,
But a ship a-sailing,
A-sailing with the wind.

One said it was a ship,
The other he said, Nay;
The third said it was a house,
With the chimney blown away.

And all the night they hunted
And nothing could they find,
But the moon a-gliding,
A-gliding with the wind.

One said it was the moon,
The other he said, Nay;
The third said it was a cheese,
And half of it cut away.

And all the day they hunted
And nothing could they find,
But a hedgehog in a bramble bush,
And that they left behind.

The first said it was a hedgehog,
The second he said, Nay;
The third said it was a pincushion,
And the pins stuck in wrong way.

And all the night they hunted
And nothing could they find,
But a hare in a turnip field,
And that they left behind.

The first said it was a hare,
The second he said, Nay;
The third said it was a calf,
And the cow had run away.

And all the day they hunted
And nothing could they find,
But an owl in a holly tree,
And that they left behind.

One said it was an owl,
The other he said, Nay;
The third said 'twas an old man,
And his beard growing grey.

R ock-a-bye baby,
Thy cradle is green,
Father's a nobleman,
Mother's a queen;
And Betty's a lady,
And wears a gold ring;
And Johnny's a drummer,
And drums for the king.

There was an old woman tossed up in a basket,
Seventeen times as high as the moon;
Where she was going I couldn't but ask it,
For in her hand she carried a broom.
Old woman, old woman, old woman, quoth I,
Where are you going to up so high?
To brush the cobwebs off the sky!
May I go with you?
Aye, by-and-by.

Little Jack Horner
Sat in the corner,
Eating a Christmas pie;
He put in his thumb,
And pulled out a plum,
And said, What a good boy am I!

Baa, baa, black sheep,
Have you any wool?
Yes, sir, yes, sir,
Three bags full;
One for the master,
And one for the dame,
And one for the little boy
Who lives down the lane.

R ing-a-ring o' roses,
A pocket full of posies,
A-tishoo! A-tishoo!
We all fall down.

Barber, barber, shave a pig,
How many hairs will make a wig?
Four and twenty, that's enough.
Give the barber a pinch of snuff.

Here am I,
Little Jumping Joan;
When nobody's with me
I'm all alone.

There were two birds sat on a stone,
Fa, la, la, la, lal, de;
One flew away, and then there was one,
Fa, la, la, la, lal, de;
The other flew after, and then there was none,
Fa, la, la, la, lal, de;
And so the poor stone was left all alone,
Fa, la, la, la, lal, de.

Hob, shoe, hob,
Hob, shoe, hob,
Here a nail,
And there a nail,
And that's well shod.

Diddle, diddle, dumpling, my son John,
Went to bed with his trousers on;
One shoe off, and one shoe on,
Diddle, diddle, dumpling, my son John.

Handy Spandy, Jack-a-Dandy,
Loves plum cake and sugar candy;
He bought some at a grocer's shop,
And out he came, hop, hop, hop, hop.

A wise old owl lived in an oak;
The more he saw the less he spoke;
The less he spoke the more he heard.
Why can't we all be like that wise old bird?

A man in the wilderness asked me,
How many strawberries grow in the sea?
I answered him, as I thought good,
As many as red herrings grow in the wood.

Where are you going to, my pretty maid?
I'm going a-milking, sir, she said,
Sir, she said, sir, she said,
I'm going a-milking, sir, she said.

May I go with you, my pretty maid?
You're kindly welcome, sir, she said,
Sir, she said, sir, she said,
You're kindly welcome, sir, she said.

Say, will you marry me, my pretty maid?
Yes, if you please, kind sir, she said,
Sir, she said, sir, she said,
Yes, if you please, kind sir, she said.

What is your father, my pretty maid?
My father's a farmer, sir, she said,
Sir, she said, sir, she said,
My father's a farmer, sir, she said.

What is your fortune, my pretty maid?
My face is my fortune, sir, she said,
Sir, she said, sir, she said,
My face is my fortune, sir, she said.

Then I can't marry you, my pretty maid.
Nobody asked you, sir, she said,
Sir, she said, sir, she said,
Nobody asked you, sir, she said.

The cat sat asleep by the side of the fire,
The mistress snored loud as a pig;
Jack took up his fiddle by Jenny's desire,
And struck up a bit of a jig.

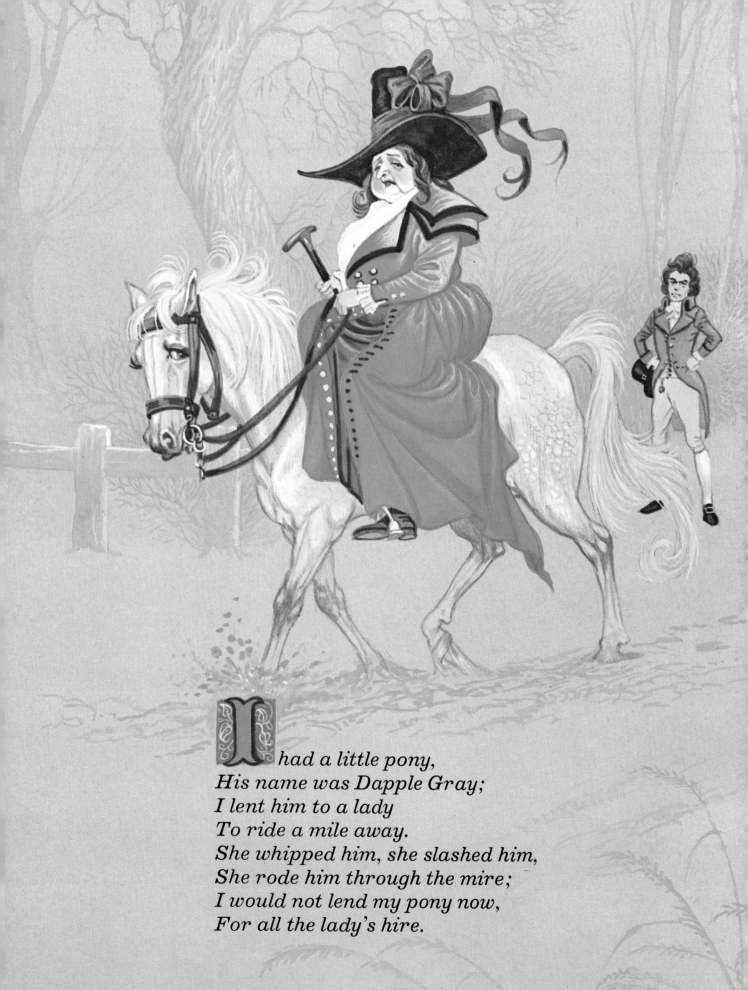

I had a little pony,
His name was Dapple Gray;
I lent him to a lady
To ride a mile away.
She whipped him, she slashed him,
She rode him through the mire;
I would not lend my pony now,
For all the lady's hire.

Twinkle, twinkle, little star,
How I wonder what you are!
Up above the world so high,
Like a diamond in the sky.

When the blazing sun is gone,
When he nothing shines upon,
Then you show your little light,
Twinkle, twinkle, all the night.

Then the traveller in the dark,
Thanks you for your tiny spark,
He could not see which way to go,
If you did not twinkle so.

In the dark blue sky you keep,
And often through my curtains peep,
For you never shut your eye,
'Till the sun is in the sky.

As your bright and tiny spark,
Lights the traveller in the dark,
Though I know not what you are,
Twinkle, twinkle, little star.

There was a piper had a cow,
And he had nought to give her.
He pulled out his pipes and played her a tune,
And bade the cow consider.

The cow considered very well
And gave the piper a penny,
And bade him play the other tune,
'Corn rigs are bonny'.

Monday's child is fair of face,

Tuesday's child is full of grace,

Wednesday's child is full of woe,

Thursday's child has far to go,

Friday's child is loving and giving,

Saturday's child works hard for his living,

And the child that is born on the Sabbath day
Is bonny and blithe, and good and gay.

83

The Man in the Moon was caught in a trap
For stealing the thorns from another man's gap.
If he had gone by, and let the thorns lie,
He'd never been Man in the Moon so high.

There was a little boy went into a barn,
And lay down on some hay;
An owl came out and flew about,
And the little boy ran away.

Pat-a-cake, pat-a-cake, baker's man,
Bake me a cake as fast as you can;
Pat it and prick it, and mark it with B,
Put it in the oven for baby and me.

The lion and the unicorn
Were fighting for the crown;
The lion beat the unicorn
All round about the town.

Some gave them white bread,
And some gave them brown;
Some gave them plum cake
And drummed them out of town.

Little King Pippin he built a fine hall,
Pie-crust and pastry-crust that was the wall;
The windows were made of black pudding and white,
And slated with pancakes, you ne'er saw the like.

Little Tommy Tucker,
Sings for his supper:
What shall we give him?
White bread and butter.
How shall he cut it
Without a knife?
How will he be married
Without a wife?

89

Cock a doodle doo!
My dame has lost her shoe,
My master's lost his fiddlestick,
And knows not what to do.

Jenny Wren fell sick
Upon a merry time,
In came Robin Redbreast
And brought her sops and wine.

Eat well of the sop, Jenny,
Drink well of the wine.
Thank you, Robin, kindly,
You shall be mine.

Jenny Wren got well,
And stood upon her feet;
And told Robin plainly,
She loved him not a bit.

Robin he got angry,
And hopped upon a twig,
Saying, Out upon you, fie upon you!
Bold faced jig!

91

Two little dicky birds,
Sitting on a wall;
One named Peter,
The other named Paul.

Fly away, Peter!
Fly away, Paul!

Come back, Peter!
Come back, Paul!

Polly put the kettle on,
Polly put the kettle on,
Polly put the kettle on,
We'll all have tea.

Sukey take it off again,
Sukey take it off again,
Sukey take it off again,
They've all gone away.

When I was a little boy
I had but little wit;
'Tis a long time ago,
And I have no more yet;
Nor ever, ever shall
Until that I die,
For the longer I live
The more fool am I.

The first day of Christmas,
My true love sent to me
A partridge in a pear tree.

The second day of Christmas,
My true love sent to me
Two turtle doves, and
A partridge in a pear tree.

The third day of Christmas,
My true love sent to me
Three French hens,
Two turtle doves, and
A partridge in a pear tree.

The fourth day of Christmas,
My true love sent to me
Four colly birds,
Three French hens,
Two turtle doves, and
A partridge in a pear tree.

The fifth day of Christmas,
My true love sent to me
Five gold rings,
Four colly birds,
Three French hens,
Two turtle doves, and
A partridge in a pear tree.

The sixth day of Christmas,
My true love sent to me
Six geese a-laying,
Five gold rings,
Four colly birds,
Three French hens,
Two turtle doves, and
A partridge in a pear tree.

The seventh day of Christmas,
My true love sent to me
Seven swans a-swimming,
Six geese a-laying,
Five gold rings,
Four colly birds,
Three French hens,
Two turtle doves, and
A partridge in a pear tree.

The eighth day of Christmas,
My true love sent to me
Eight maids a-milking,
Seven swans a-swimming,
Six geese a-laying,
Five gold rings,
Four colly birds,
Three French hens,
Two turtle doves, and
A partridge in a pear tree.

The ninth day of Christmas,
My true love sent to me
Nine drummers drumming,
Eight maids a-milking,
Seven swans a-swimming,
Six geese a-laying,
Five gold rings,
Four colly birds,
Three French hens,
Two turtle doves, and
A partridge in a pear tree.

The tenth day of Christmas,
My true love sent to me
Ten pipers piping,
Nine drummers drumming,
Eight maids a-milking,
Seven swans a-swimming,
Six geese a-laying,
Five gold rings,
Four colly birds,
Three French hens,
Two turtle doves, and
A partridge in a pear tree.

97

The eleventh day of Christmas,
My true love sent to me
Eleven ladies dancing,
Ten pipers piping,
Nine drummers drumming,
Eight maids a-milking,
Seven swans a-swimming,
Six geese a-laying,
Five gold rings,
Four colly birds,
Three French hens,
Two turtle doves, and
A partridge in a pear tree.

The twelfth day of Christmas,
My true love sent to me
Twelve lords a-leaping,
Eleven ladies dancing,
Ten pipers piping,
Nine drummers drumming,
Eight maids a-milking,
Seven swans a-swimming,
Six geese a-laying,
Five gold rings,
Four colly birds,
Three French hens,
Two turtle doves, and
A partridge in a pear tree.

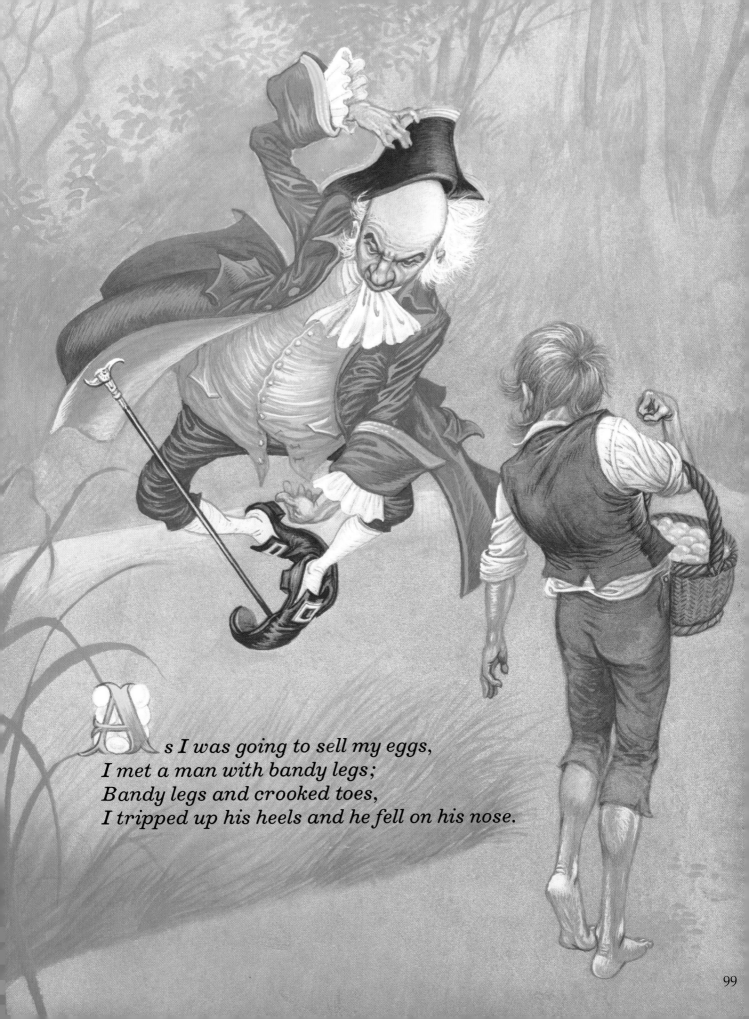

As I was going to sell my eggs,
I met a man with bandy legs;
Bandy legs and crooked toes,
I tripped up his heels and he fell on his nose.

Brow bender,
Eye peeper,
Nose dreeper,
Mouth eater,
Chin chopper,
Knock at the door,
Ring the bell,
Lift up the latch,
Walk in . . .
Take a chair,
Sit by there,
How d'you do this morning?

Three young rats with black felt hats,
Three young ducks with white straw flats,
Three young dogs with curling tails,
Three young cats with demi-veils,
Went out to walk with two young pigs
In satin vests and sorrel wigs.
But suddenly it chanced to rain
And so they all went home again.

I went into my grandmother's garden,
And there I found a farthing.
I went into my next door neighbour's;
There I bought a pipkin and a popkin,
A slipkin and a slopkin,
A nailboard, a sailboard,
And all for a farthing.

As a little fat man of Bombay
Was smoking one very hot day,
A bird called a snipe
Flew away with his pipe,
Which vexed the fat man of Bombay.

Jack be nimble,
Jack be quick,
Jack jump over
The candle stick.

103

Solomon Grundy,
Born on a Monday,
Christened on Tuesday,
Married on Wednesday,
Took ill on Thursday,
Worse on Friday,
Died on Saturday,
Buried on Sunday.
This is the end
Of Solomon Grundy.

There was an old woman
Sold puddings and pies;
She went to the mill
And dust blew in her eyes.
She has hot pies
And cold pies to sell;
Wherever she goes
You may follow her by the smell.

Sing a song of sixpence,
A pocket full of rye;
Four and twenty blackbirds,
Baked in a pie.

When the pie was opened,
The birds began to sing;
Was not that a dainty dish,
To set before the king?

The king was in his counting house,
Counting out his money;
The queen was in the parlour,
Eating bread and honey.

The maid was in the garden,
Hanging out the clothes,
There came a little blackbird,
And snapped off her nose.

If I had a donkey that wouldn't go,
Would I beat him? Oh no, no.
I'd put him in the barn and give him some corn,
The best little donkey that ever was born.

Tommy Trot a man of law,
Sold his bed and lay upon straw;
Sold the straw and slept on grass,
To buy his wife a looking glass.

Hey diddle diddle,
The cat and the fiddle,
The cow jumped over the moon;
The little dog laughed
To see such sport,
And the dish ran away with the spoon.

Higglety, pigglety, pop!
The dog has eaten the mop;
The pig's in a hurry,
The cat's in a flurry,
Higglety, pigglety, pop!

A farmer went trotting upon his grey mare,
Bumpety, bumpety, bump!
With his daughter behind him so rosy and fair,
Lumpety, lumpety, lump!

A raven cried, Croak! and they all tumbled down,
Bumpety, bumpety, bump!
The mare broke her knees and the farmer his crown,
Lumpety, lumpety, lump!

The mischievous raven flew laughing away,
Bumpety, bumpety, bump!
And vowed he would serve them the same next day,
Lumpety, lumpety, lump!

Robin and Richard
Were two pretty men,
They lay in bed
Till the clock struck ten
Then up starts Robin
And looks at the sky,
Oh, brother Richard,
The sun's very high.
You go before
With the bottle and bag,
And I will come after
On little Jack Nag.

Ding, dong, bell,
Pussy's in the well.
Who put her in?
Little Johnny Green.
Who pulled her out?
Little Tommy Stout.
What a naughty boy was that,
To try to drown poor pussy cat,
Who never did him any harm,
And killed the mice in his father's barn.

Yankee Doodle came to town,
Riding on a pony;
He stuck a feather in his cap
And called it macaroni.

Old Mother Hubbard
Went to the cupboard,
To fetch her poor dog a bone;
But when she came there
The cupboard was bare
And so the poor dog had none.

She went to the baker's
To buy him some bread;
But when she came back
The poor dog was dead.

She went to the undertaker's
To buy him a coffin;
But when she came back
The poor dog was laughing.

She took a clean dish
To get him some tripe;
But when she came back
He was smoking a pipe.

She went to the alehouse
To get him some beer;
But when she came back
The dog sat in a chair.

She went to the tavern
For white wine and red;
But when she came back
The dog stood on his head.

She went to the fruiterer's
To buy him some fruit;
But when she came back
He was playing the flute.

She went to the tailor's
To buy him a coat;
But when she came back
He was riding a goat.

She went to the hatter's
To buy him a hat;
But when she came back
He was feeding the cat.

She went to the barber's
To buy him a wig;
But when she came back
He was dancing a jig.

She went to the cobbler's
To buy him some shoes;
But when she came back
He was reading the news.

She went to the seamstress
To buy him some linen;
But when she came back
The dog was a-spinning.

She went to the hosier's
To buy him some hose;
But when she came back
He was dressed in his clothes.

The dame made a curtsy,
The dog made a bow;
The dame said, Your servant,
The dog said, Bow-wow.

Gregory Griggs, Gregory Griggs,
Had twenty seven different wigs.
He wore them up, he wore them down,
To please the people of the town;
He wore them east, he wore them west,
But he never could tell which he loved the best.

R ub-a-dub-dub,
Three men in a tub,
And how do you think they got there?
The butcher, the baker,
The candlestick-maker,
They all jumped out of a rotten potato,
'Twas enough to make a man stare.

O ne misty, moisty, morning,
When cloudy was the weather,
There I met an old man
Clothed all in leather;
Clothed all in leather,
With cap under his chin.
How do you do, and how do you do,
And how do you do again?

119

There was a man, and his name was Dob,
And he had a wife, and her name was Mob,
And he had a dog, and he called it Cob,
And she had a cat, called Chitterabob.
Cob, says Dob,
Chitterabob, says Mob.
Cob was Dob's dog,
Chitterabob Mob's cat.

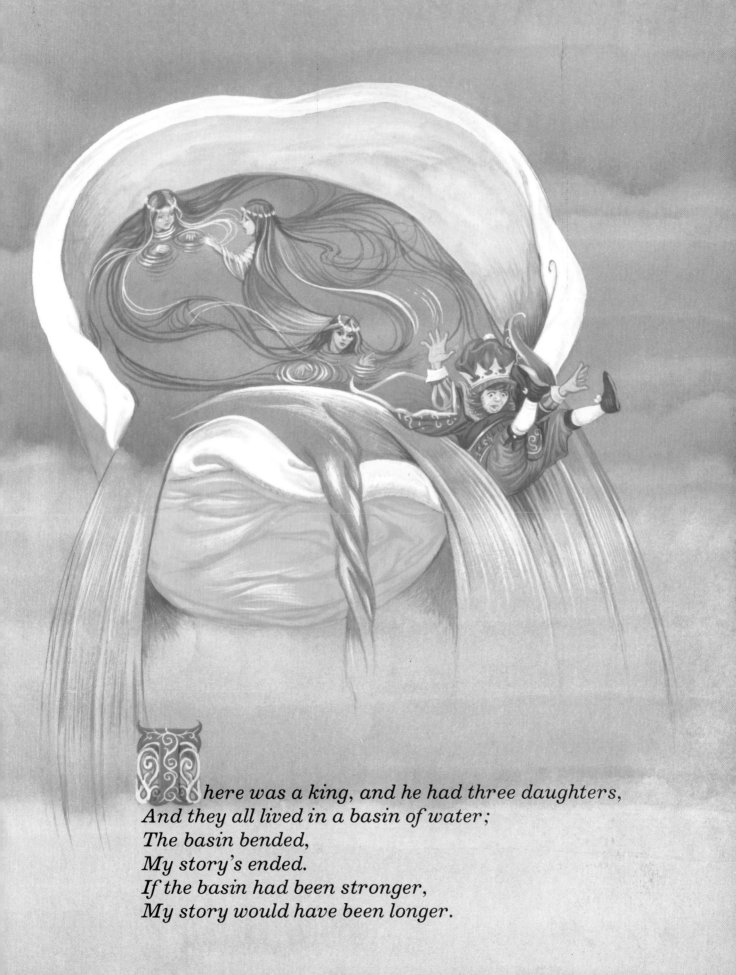

There was a king, and he had three daughters,
And they all lived in a basin of water;
The basin bended,
My story's ended.
If the basin had been stronger,
My story would have been longer.

There was a jolly miller once,
Lived on the river Dee;
He worked and sang from morn till night,
No lark more blithe than he.
And this the burden of his song
Forever used to be,
I care for nobody, no! not I,
If nobody cares for me.

Oranges and lemons,
Say the bells of St. Clement's.

You owe me five farthings,
Say the bells of St. Martin's.

When will you pay me?
Say the bells of Old Bailey.

When I grow rich,
Say the bells of Shoreditch.

When will that be?
Say the bells of Stepney.

I'm sure I don't know,
Says the great bell at Bow.

Here comes a candle to light you to bed,
Here comes a chopper to chop off your head.

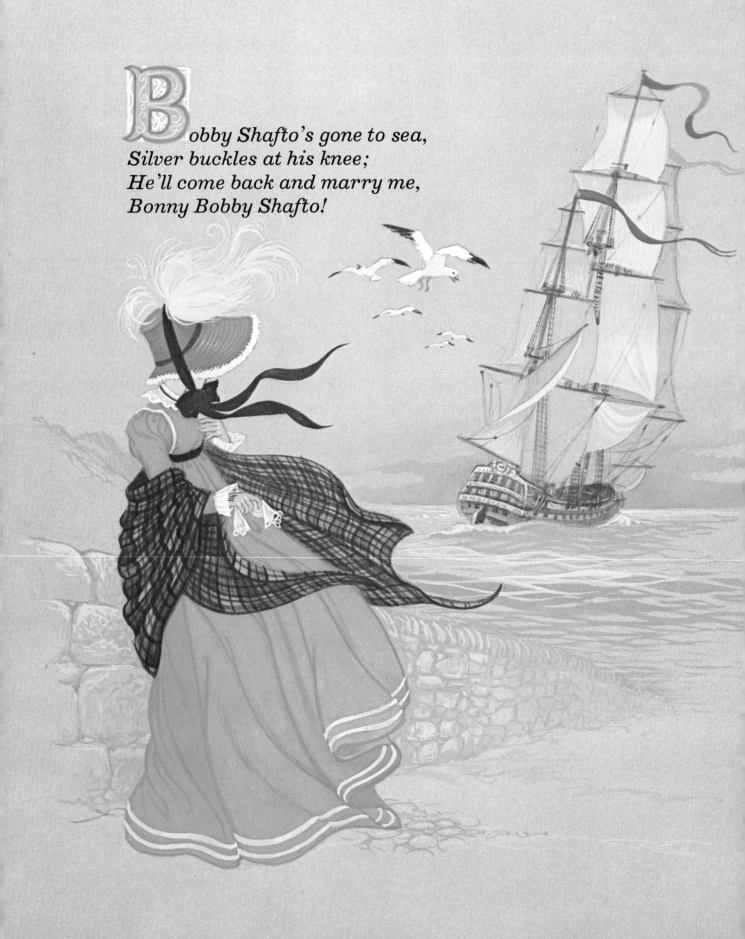

Bobby Shafto's gone to sea,
Silver buckles at his knee;
He'll come back and marry me,
Bonny Bobby Shafto!

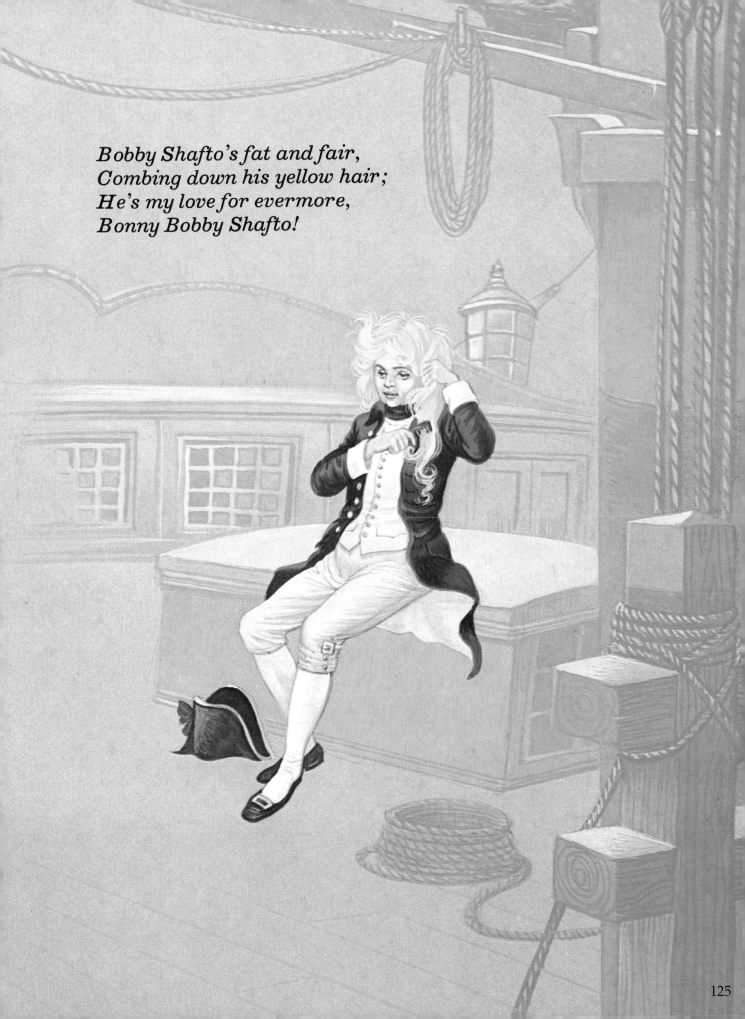

Bobby Shafto's fat and fair,
Combing down his yellow hair;
He's my love for evermore,
Bonny Bobby Shafto!

Boys and girls come out to play,
The moon doth shine as bright as day.
    Leave your supper and leave your sleep,
And join your playfellows in the street.
    Come with a whoop and come with a call,
Come with a good will or not at all.
    Up the ladder and down the wall,
A half-penny loaf will serve us all;
    You find milk, and I'll find flour,
And we'll have a pudding in half an hour.

Pussy cat, pussy cat, where have you been?
I've been to London to look at the queen.
Pussy cat, pussy cat, what did you there?
I frightened a little mouse under her chair.

Wee Willie Winkie runs through the town,
Upstairs and downstairs in his night-gown,
Rapping at the window, crying through the lock,
Are the children all in bed, for now it's eight o'clock?

Ride a cock-horse to Banbury Cross,
To see a fine lady upon a white horse;
Rings on her fingers and bells on her toes,
And she shall have music wherever she goes.

127

Pease porridge hot,
Pease porridge cold,
Pease porridge in the pot
Nine days old.

Some like it hot,
Some like it cold,
Some like it in the pot
Nine days old.

There was an old woman
Who lived in Dundee,
And in her back garden
There grew a plum tree;
The plums they grew rotten
Before they grew ripe,
And she sold them three farthings a pint.

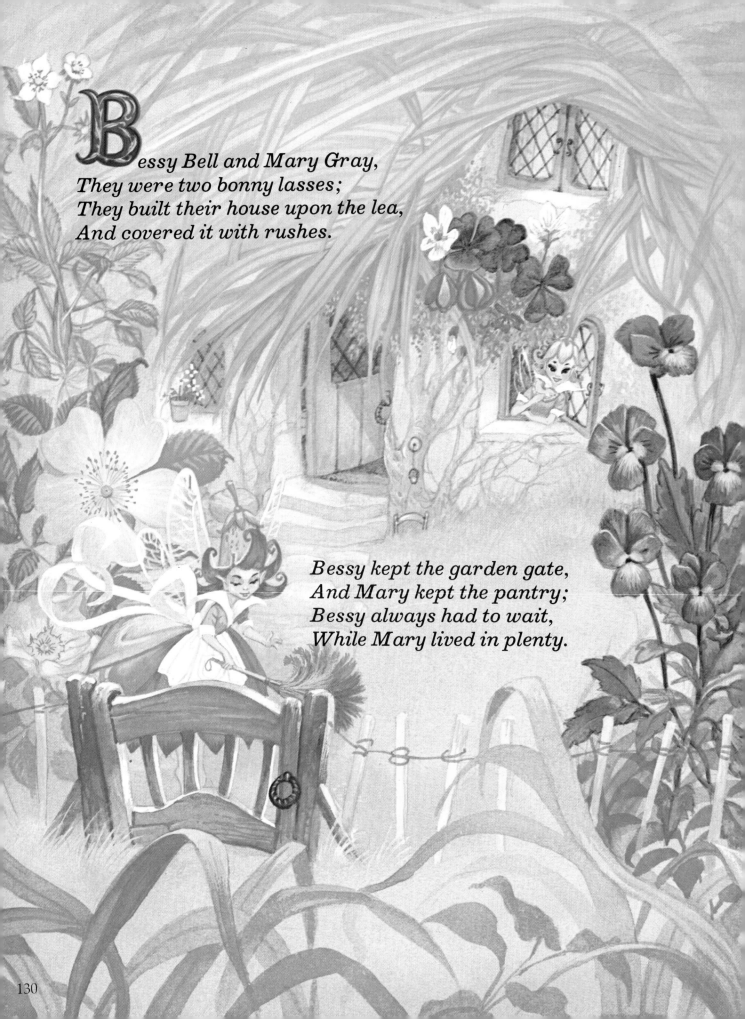

Bessy Bell and Mary Gray,
They were two bonny lasses;
They built their house upon the lea,
And covered it with rushes.

Bessy kept the garden gate,
And Mary kept the pantry;
Bessy always had to wait,
While Mary lived in plenty.

I do not like thee, Doctor Fell,
The reason why I cannot tell;
But this I know, and know full well,
I do not like thee, Doctor Fell.

The fiddler and his wife,
The piper and his mother,
Ate three half-cakes, three whole cakes,
And three quarters of another.

I had a little hobby horse, it was well shod,
It carried me to London, niddety nod,
And when we got to London we heard a great shout,
Down fell my hobby horse and I cried out:
Up again, hobby horse, if thou be a beast,
When we get to our town we will have a feast,
And if there is but little, why thou shalt have some,
And dance to the bag-pipes and beating of the drum.

A cat came fiddling out of a barn,
With a pair of bag-pipes under her arm;
She could sing nothing but, Fiddle cum fee,
The mouse has married the humble-bee.
Pipe cat; dance, mouse;
We'll have a wedding at our good house.

133

The north wind doth blow,
And we shall have snow,
And what will poor robin do then?
Poor thing.
He'll sit in a barn,
And keep himself warm,
And hide his head under his wing.
Poor thing.

Six little mice sat down to spin;
Pussy passed by and she peeped in.
What are you doing, my little men?
Weaving coats for gentlemen.
Shall I come in and cut off your threads?
No, no, Mistress Pussy, you'd bite off our heads.
Oh no, I'll not; I'll help you to spin.
That may be so, but you don't come in.

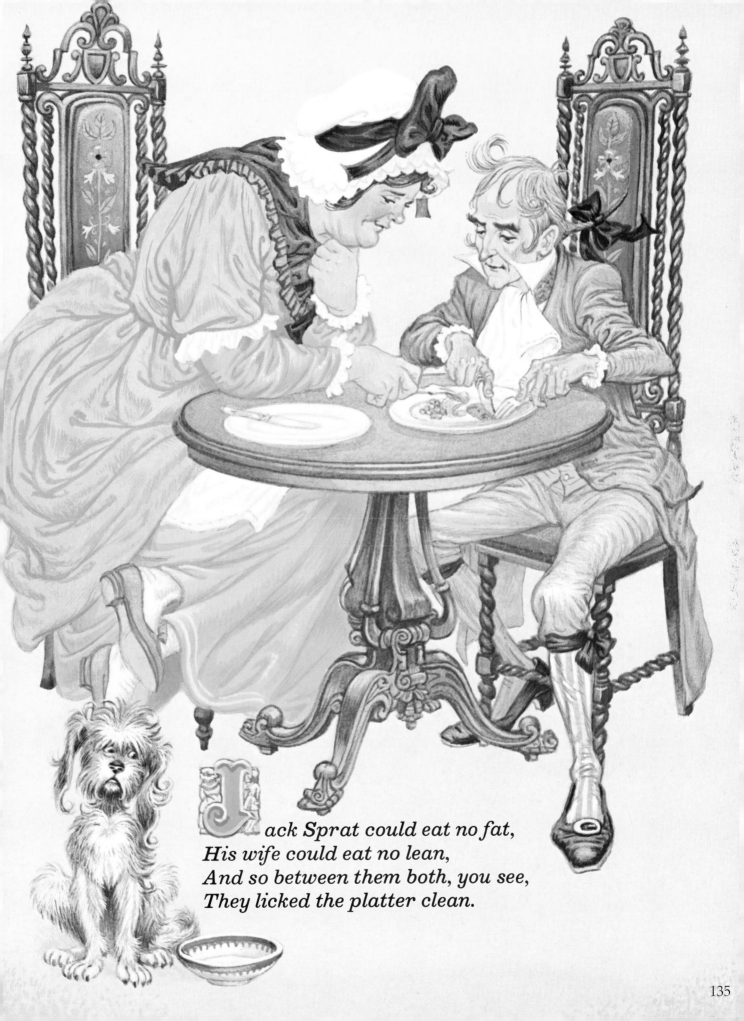

Jack Sprat could eat no fat,
His wife could eat no lean,
And so between them both, you see,
They licked the platter clean.

135

When Good King Arthur ruled this land,
He was a goodly king;
He stole three pecks of barley-meal
To make a bag-pudding.

A bag-pudding the king did make,
And stuffed it well with plums;
And in it put great lumps of fat,
As big as my two thumbs.

The king and queen did eat thereof,
And noblemen beside;
And what they could not eat that night,
The queen next morning fried.

Oh where, oh where has my little dog gone?
Oh where, oh where can he be?
With his ears cut short and his tail cut long,
Oh where, oh where is he?

Who killed Cock Robin?
I, said the Sparrow,
With my bow and arrow,
I killed Cock Robin.

Who saw him die?
I, said the Fly,
With my little eye,
I saw him die.

Who caught his blood?
I, said the Fish,
With my little dish,
I caught his blood.

Who'll make the shroud?
I, said the Beetle,
With my thread and needle,
I'll make the shroud.

Who'll dig his grave?
I, said the Owl,
With my pick and shovel,
I'll dig his grave.

Who'll be the parson?
I, said the Rook,
With my little book,
I'll be the parson.

Who'll be the clerk?
I, said the Lark,
If it's not in the dark,
I'll be the clerk.

Who'll carry the link?
I, said the Linnet,
I'll fetch it in a minute,
I'll carry the link.

Who'll be chief mourner?
I, said the Dove,
I mourn for my love,
I'll be chief mourner.

Who'll carry the coffin?
I, said the Kite,
If it's not through the night,
I'll carry the coffin.

Who'll bear the pall?
We, said the Wren,
Both the cock and the hen,
We'll bear the pall.

Who'll sing a psalm?
I, said the Thrush,
As she sat on a bush,
I'll sing a psalm.

Who'll toll the bell?
I, said the Bull,
Because I can pull,
I'll toll the bell.

All the birds of the air
Fell a-sighing and a-sobbing,
When they heard the bell toll
For poor Cock Robin.

Punch and Judy
Fought for a pie;
Punch gave Judy
A knock in the eye.
Says Punch to Judy
Will you have any more?
Says Judy to Punch,
My eye is sore.

Bow, wow, wow,
Whose dog art thou?
Little Tom Tinker's dog,
Bow, wow, wow.

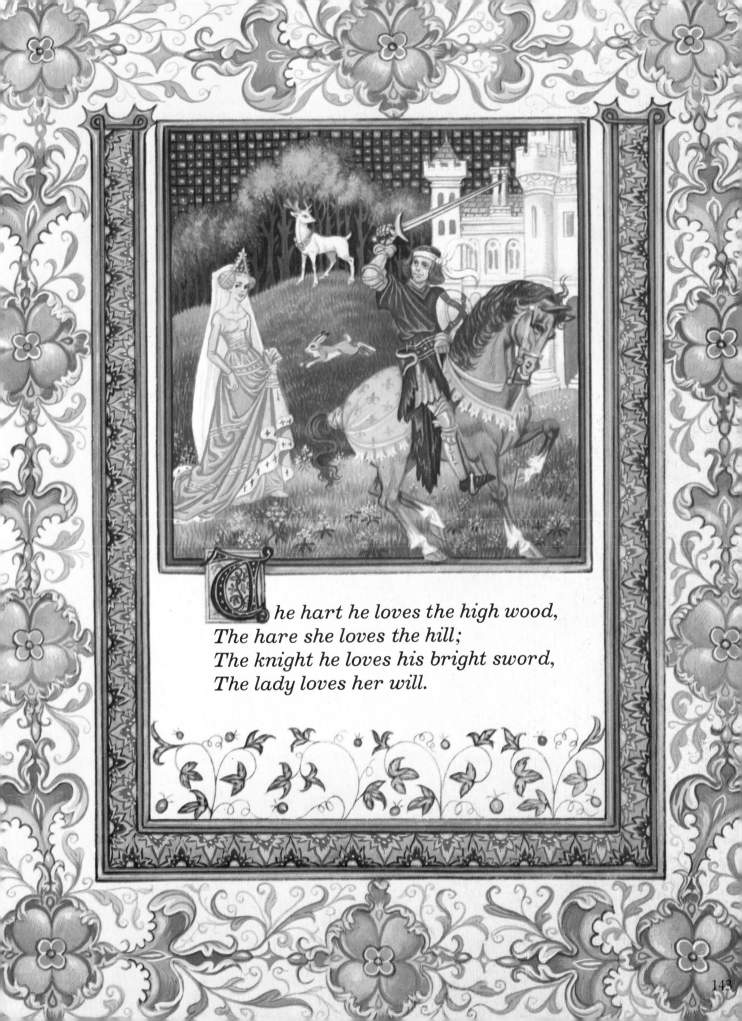

The hart he loves the high wood,
The hare she loves the hill;
The knight he loves his bright sword,
The lady loves her will.

Cackle, cackle, Mother Goose,
Have you any feathers loose?
Truly have I, pretty fellow,
Half enough to fill a pillow.
Here are quills, take one or two,
And down to make a bed for you.

Little Polly Flinders
Sat among the cinders,
Warming her pretty little toes;
Her mother came and caught her,
And whipped her little daughter
For spoiling her nice new clothes.

This little pig went to market,
This little pig stayed at home,
This little pig had roast beef,
This little pig had none,
And this little pig cried, Wee-wee-wee-wee-wee,
I can't find my way home.

Mr Ibister, and Betsy his sister,
Resolved upon giving a treat;
So letters they write,
Their friends to invite,
To their house in Great Camomile Street.

Sing, sing, what shall I sing?
The cat's run away with the pudding-string!
Do, do, what shall I do?
The cat has bitten it quite in two.

Tweedledum and Tweedledee
Agreed to have a battle,
For Tweedledum said Tweedledee
Had spoiled his nice new rattle.
Just then flew by a monstrous crow,
As big as a tar-barrel,
Which frightened both the heroes so,
They quite forgot their quarrel.

Tom, Tom, the piper's son,
Stole a pig and away he run;
The pig was eat
And Tom was beat,
And Tom went howling down the street.

I saw three ships come sailing by,
Come sailing by, come sailing by,
I saw three ships come sailing by,
On New-Year's day in the morning.

And what do you think was in them then,
Was in them then, was in them then?
And what do you think was in them then,
On New-Year's day in the morning?

Three pretty girls were in them then,
Were in them then, were in them then,
Three pretty girls were in them then,
On New-Year's day in the morning.

One could whistle, and one could sing,
And one could play on the violin;
Such joy there was at my wedding,
On New-Year's day in the morning.

There was an old woman who lived in a shoe,
She had so many children she didn't know what to do;
She gave them some broth without any bread;
She whipped them all soundly and put them to bed.

Ladybird, ladybird,
Fly away home,
Your house is on fire
And your children all gone;
All except one
And that's little Ann
And she has crept under
The warming pan.

See-saw, Margery Daw,
Jacky shall have a new master;
Jacky shall have but a penny a day,
Because he can't work any faster.

Old Mother Shuttle
Lived in a coal-scuttle
Along with her dog and her cat;
What they ate I can't tell,
But 'tis known very well
That not one of the party was fat.

Old Mother Shuttle
Scoured out her coal-scuttle,
And washed both her dog and her cat;
The cat scratched her nose,
So they came to hard blows,
And who was the gainer by that?

Mr. East gave a feast;
Mr. North laid the cloth;
Mr. West did his best;
Mr. South burnt his mouth
With eating a cold potato.

Cobbler, cobbler, mend my shoe.
Yes, good master, that I'll do;
Here's my awl and wax and thread,
And now your shoe is quite mended.

There was a crooked man, and he walked a crooked mile,
He found a crooked sixpence against a crooked stile;
He bought a crooked cat,
which caught a crooked mouse,
And they all lived together in a little crooked house.

157

I saw a ship a-sailing,
A-sailing on the sea,
And oh but it was laden
With pretty things for thee.

There were comfits in the cabin,
And apples in the hold;
The sails were made of silk,
And the masts were all of gold.

The four-and-twenty sailors,
That stood between the decks,
Were four-and-twenty white mice
With chains about their necks.

The captain was a duck
With a packet on his back,
And when the ship began to move
The captain said Quack! Quack!

The Queen of Hearts
She made some tarts,
All on a summer's day;
The Knave of Hearts
He stole the tarts,
And took them clean away.

The King of Hearts
Called for the tarts,
And beat the knave full sore;
The Knave of Hearts
Brought back the tarts,
And vowed he'd steal no more.

I had a little nut tree,
Nothing would it bear
But a silver nutmeg
And a golden pear;

The King of Spain's daughter
Came to visit me,
And all for the sake
Of my little nut tree.

*H*ey diddle dinkety, poppety, pet,
The merchants of London they wear scarlet;
Silk in the collar and gold in the hem,
So merrily march the merchant men.

*L*ittle Nancy Etticoat,
With a white petticoat,
And a red nose;
She has no feet or hands,
The longer she stands
The shorter she grows.

One, two,
Buckle my shoe;
Three, four,
Knock at the door;
Five, six,
Pick up sticks;
Seven, eight,
Lay them straight;
Nine, ten,
A big fat hen;
Eleven, twelve,
Dig and delve;
Thirteen, fourteen,
Maids a-courting;
Fifteen, sixteen,
Maids in the kitchen;
Seventeen, eighteen,
Maids in waiting;
Nineteen, twenty,
My plate's empty.

Little Bo-peep has lost her sheep,
And can't tell where to find them;
Leave them alone, and they'll come home,
And bring their tails behind them.

Little Bo-peep fell fast asleep,
And dreamt she heard them bleating;
But when she awoke, she found it a joke,
For they were still all fleeting.

Then up she took her little crook,
Determined for to find them;
She found them indeed, but it made her heart bleed,
For they'd left their tails behind them.

It happened one day, as Bo-peep did stray
Into a meadow hard by,
There she espied their tails side by side,
All hung on a tree to dry.

She heaved a sigh, and wiped her eye,
And over the hillocks went rambling,
And tried what she could, as a shepherdess should,
To tack again each to its lambkin.

164

Peter Piper picked a peck of pickled pepper;
A peck of pickled pepper Peter Piper picked;
If Peter Piper picked a peck of pickled pepper,
Where's the peck of pickled pepper Peter Piper picked?

There was a little girl, and she had a little curl
Right in the middle of her forehead;
When she was good, she was very, very good,
But when she was bad, she was horrid.

When I was a little boy I lived by myself,
And all the bread and cheese I got I laid upon a shelf;
The rats and the mice they made such a strife,
I had to go to London town and buy me a wife.

The streets were so broad and the lanes were so narrow,
I was forced to bring my wife home in a wheelbarrow.
The wheelbarrow broke and my wife had a fall,
Farewell wheelbarrow, little wife and all.

There was a monkey climbed a tree,
When he fell down, then down fell he.

There was a crow sat on a stone,
When he was gone, then there was none.

There was an old wife did eat an apple,
When she ate two, she ate a couple.

There was a horse going to the mill,
When he went on, he stood not still.

There was a butcher cut his thumb,
When it did bleed, then blood did come.

There was a lackey ran a race,
When he ran fast, he ran apace.

There was a cobbler clouting shoon,
When they were mended, they were done.

There was a chandler making candle,
When he them stripped, he did them handle.

There was a navy went to Spain,
When it returned, it came again.

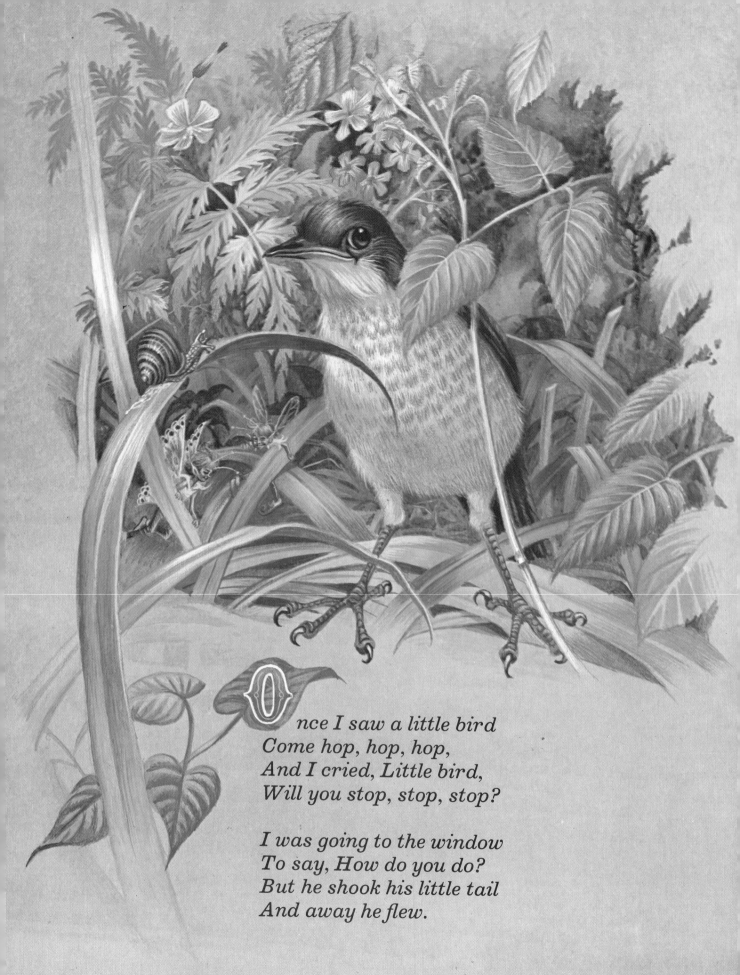

Once I saw a little bird
Come hop, hop, hop,
And I cried, Little bird,
Will you stop, stop, stop?

I was going to the window
To say, How do you do?
But he shook his little tail
And away he flew.

170

Little Boy Blue,
Come blow your horn,
The sheep's in the meadow,
The cow's in the corn;
But where is the boy
Who looks after the sheep?
He's under a haystack,
Fast asleep.
Will you wake him?
No, not I,
For if I do,
He's sure to cry.

Bell horses, bell horses,
What time of day?
One o'clock, two o'clock,
Time to away.

This is the house that Jack built.

This is the malt
That lay in the house that Jack built.

This is the rat,
That ate the malt
That lay in the house that Jack built.

This is the cat,
That killed the rat,
That ate the malt
That lay in the house that Jack built.

This is the dog,
That worried the cat,
That killed the rat,
That ate the malt
That lay in the house that Jack built.

This is the cow with the crumpled horn,
That tossed the dog,
That worried the cat,
That killed the rat,
That ate the malt
That lay in the house that Jack built.

This is the maiden all forlorn,
That milked the cow with the crumpled horn,
That tossed the dog,
That worried the cat,
That killed the rat,
That ate the malt
That lay in the house that Jack built.

This is the man all tattered and torn,
That kissed the maiden all forlorn,
That milked the cow with the crumpled horn,
That tossed the dog,
That worried the cat,
That killed the rat,
That ate the malt
That lay in the house that Jack built.

This is the priest all shaven and shorn,
That married the man all tattered and torn,
That kissed the maiden all forlorn,
That milked the cow with the crumpled horn,
That tossed the dog,
That worried the cat,
That killed the rat,
That ate the malt
That lay in the house that Jack built.

This is the cock that crowed in the morn,
That waked the priest all shaven and shorn,
That married the man all tattered and torn,
That kissed the maiden all forlorn,
That milked the cow with the crumpled horn,
That tossed the dog,
That worried the cat,
That killed the rat,
That ate the malt
That lay in the house that Jack built.

This is the farmer sowing his corn,
That kept the cock that crowed in the morn,
That waked the priest all shaven and shorn,
That married the man all tattered and torn,
That kissed the maiden all forlorn,
That milked the cow with the crumpled horn,
That tossed the dog,
That worried the cat,
That killed the rat,
That ate the malt
That lay in the house that Jack built.

Hot cross buns!
Hot cross buns!
One a penny, two a penny,
Hot cross buns!
If your daughters do not like them
Give them to your sons;
But if you haven't any of these pretty little elves
You cannot do better than eat them yourselves.

As I walked by myself,
And talked to myself,
Myself said unto me,
Look to thyself,
Take care of thyself,
For nobody cares for thee.

I answered myself,
And said to myself,
In the self-same repartee,
Look to thyself,
Or not to thyself,
The self-same thing will be.

I had a little hobby horse
And it was dapple gray,
Its head was made of pea-straw,
Its tail was made of hay.

I sold him to an old woman
For a copper groat,
And I'll not sing my song again
Without a new coat.

There was a man and he had nought,
And robbers came to rob him;
He crept up to the chimney top,
And then they thought they had him.

But he got down on the other side,
And then they could not find him;
He ran fourteen miles in fifteen days,
And never looked behind him.

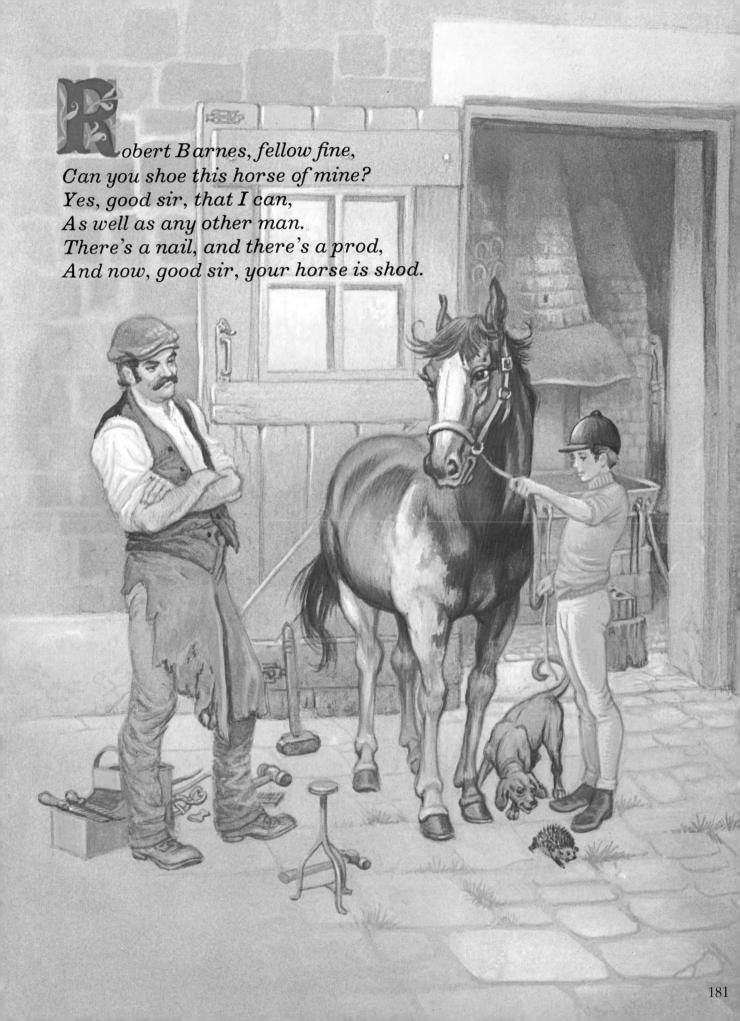

Robert Barnes, fellow fine,
Can you shoe this horse of mine?
Yes, good sir, that I can,
As well as any other man.
There's a nail, and there's a prod,
And now, good sir, your horse is shod.

Humpty Dumpty sat on a wall,
Humpty Dumpty had a great fall.
All the king's horses,
And all the king's men,
Couldn't put Humpty together again.

Hark, hark,
The dogs do bark,
The beggars are coming to town;
Some in rags,
And some in jags,
And one in a velvet gown.

Anna Elise, she jumped with surprise;
The surprise was so quick, it played her a trick;
The trick was so rare, she jumped in a chair;
The chair was so frail, she jumped in a pail;
The pail was so wet, she jumped in a net;
The net was so small, she jumped on the ball;
The ball was so round, she jumped on the ground;
And ever since then she's been turning around.

To market, to market, to buy a fat pig,
Home again, home again, jiggety-jig;
To market, to market, to buy a fat hog,
Home again, home again, jiggety-jog.

The Owl and the Pussy-cat went to sea
In a beautiful pea-green boat,
They took some honey, and plenty of money,
Wrapped up in a five-pound note.
The Owl looked up to the stars above,
And sang to a small guitar,
'O lovely Pussy! Pussy, my love,
What a beautiful Pussy you are,
        You are,
        You are!
What a beautiful Pussy you are!'

Pussy said to the Owl, 'You elegant fowl!
How charmingly sweet you sing!
O let us be married! too long we have tarried:
But what shall we do for a ring?'
They sailed away, for a year and a day,
To the land where the Bong-tree grows,
And there in a wood a Piggy-wig stood
With a ring at the end of his nose,
        His nose,
        His nose,
With a ring at the end of his nose.

'Dear Pig, are you willing to sell for one shilling
Your ring?' Said the Piggy, 'I will'.
So they took it away, and were married next day
By the Turkey who lives on the hill.
They dined on mince, and slices of quince,
Which they ate with a runcible spoon;
And hand in hand, on the edge of the sand,
They danced by the light of the moon,
        The moon,
        The moon,
They danced by the light of the moon.

Grandfa' Grig
Had a pig,
In a field of clover;
Piggie died,
Grandfa' cried,
And all the fun was over.

How many days has my baby to play?
Saturday, Sunday, Monday,
Tuesday, Wednesday, Thursday, Friday,
Saturday, Sunday, Monday.
Hop away, skip away,
My baby wants to play,
My baby wants to play every day.

Three wise men of Gotham,
They went to sea in a bowl,
And if the bowl had been stronger
My song had been longer.

As I was going up the hill,
I met with Jack the piper;
And all the tune that he could play
Was, 'Tie up your petticoats tighter'.

I tied them once, I tied them twice,
I tied them three times over;
And all the song that he could sing
Was, 'Carry me safe to Dover'.

I had a little hen,
The prettiest ever seen;
She washed up the dishes,
And kept the house clean.
She went to the mill
To fetch me some flour,
And always got home
In less than an hour.
She baked me my bread,
She brewed me my ale,
She sat by the fire
And told a fine tale.

here was an old woman of Surrey,
Who was morn, noon, and night in a hurry;
Called her husband a fool,
Drove her children to school,
The worrying old woman of Surrey.

192

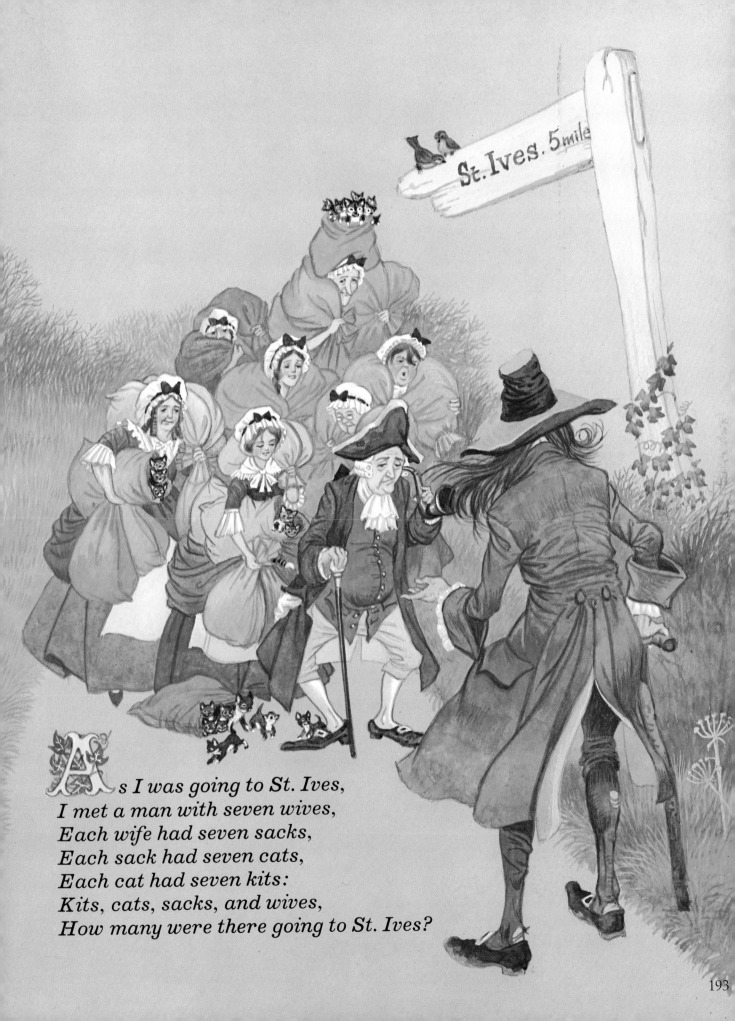

As I was going to St. Ives,
I met a man with seven wives,
Each wife had seven sacks,
Each sack had seven cats,
Each cat had seven kits:
Kits, cats, sacks, and wives,
How many were there going to St. Ives?

The sow came in with the saddle,
The little pig rocked the cradle,
The dish jumped up on the table,
To see the pot swallow the ladle.
The spit that stood behind the door
Threw the pudding-stick on the floor.
Odd's-bobs! says the gridiron,
Can't you agree?
I'm the head constable,
Bring them to me.

ary, Mary, quite contrary,
How does your garden grow?
With silver bells and cockle shells,
And pretty maids all in a row.

Hickory, dickory, dock,
The mouse ran up the clock.
The clock struck one,
The mouse ran down,
Hickory, dickory, dock.

Ride a cock-horse
To Banbury Cross,
To see what Tommy can buy;
A penny white loaf,
A penny white cake,
And a two-penny apple-pie.

I had a little husband,
No bigger than my thumb;
I put him in a pint-pot
And there I bade him drum.
I bought a little horse
That galloped up and down;
I bridled him, and saddled him
And sent him out of town.
I gave him some garters
To garter up his hose,
And a little silk handkerchief
To wipe his pretty nose.

197

Little Bob Robin,
Where do you live?
Up in yonder wood, sir,
On a hazel twig.

Little Betty Blue
Lost her holiday shoe,
What can little Betty do?
Give her another
To match the other,
And then she may walk out in two.

Little Miss Muffet
Sat on a tuffet,
Eating her curds and whey;
There came a big spider,
Who sat down beside her
And frightened Miss Muffet away.

If all the world were paper,
And all the sea were ink,
If all the trees were bread and cheese,
What should we have to drink?

ray goose and gander,
Waft your wings together
And carry the good king's daughter
Over the one-strand river.

As I was going along,
long, long,
A-singing a comical song,
song, song,
The lane that I went was so
long, long, long,
And the song that I sung
was as long, long, long,
And so I went singing along.

I had a little moppet,
I kept it in my pocket
And fed it on corn and hay;
Then came a proud beggar
And said he would wed her,
And stole my little moppet away.

The dove says, Coo, coo, what shall I do?
I can scarce maintain two.
Pooh, pooh, says the wren, I have ten,
And keep them all like gentlemen.

203

I see the moon,
And the moon sees me;
God bless the moon,
And God bless me.